This igloo book belongs to:

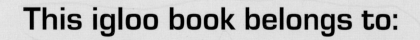

igloobooks

Published in 2014
by Igloo Books Ltd
Cottage Farm
Sywell
NN6 0BJ
www.igloobooks.com

HUN001 1014
2 4 6 8 10 9 7 5 3 1
ISBN: 978-1-78440-306-5

Printed and manufactured in China

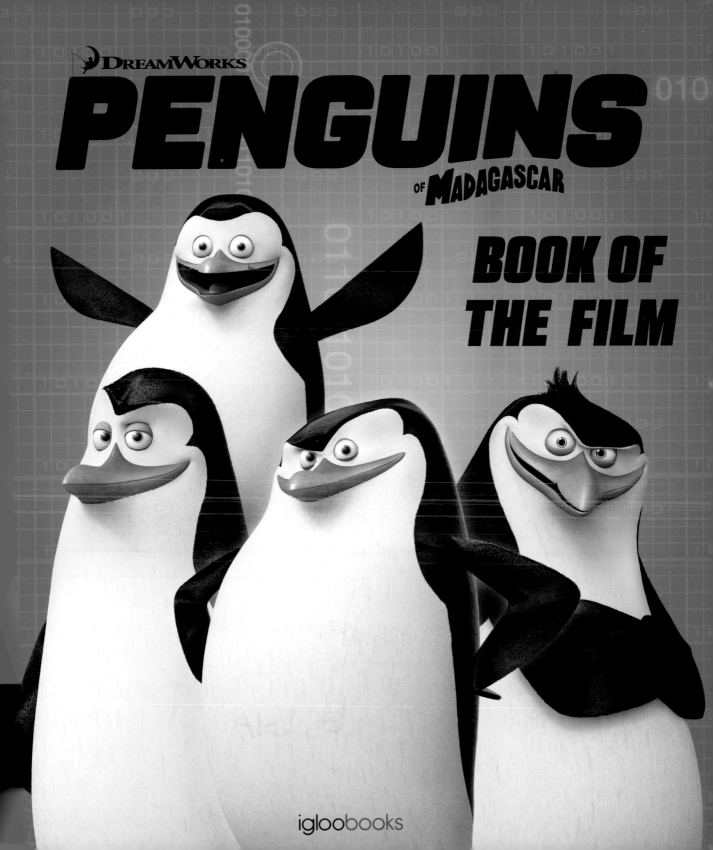

In a mysterious submarine, in Venice, Italy, a group of penguins were being held captive by an ugly, purple octopus.

"Well hello, Skipper, Rico, Kowalski and Private. We meet again," said the octopus.

"Enough with the sweet talk," said Skipper. "Now, who are you and why are we here?"

The octopus smiled.

"I... am... DAVE!" he cried. "Soon after I started life in my first aquarium, people ignored me. It was always about the cute penguins. Well not for long! I have developed a serum-firing ray machine to take away your cuteness. Soon, penguins around the world will be hideous and then people will love me."

"Not on my watch, Derek," said Skipper. The penguins wriggled free and leapt into action. In the struggle, Dave lost his grip on the serum bottle he was holding.

"Dave!" cried the octopus. "My name is Dave!"

The serum flew through the air. Rico slid to catch it, but one of Dave's tentacles caught it first. Suddenly, octopus henchmen burst in and charged at the penguins.

"Kowalski, escape route!" shouted Skipper. The penguins leapt through a hatch in the roof and found themselves on a canal. "Alright boys, just like Cuba," said Skipper.

The penguins leapt off the submarine and landed in a passing gondola.

Just then, a swarm of octopus henchmen scrambled out of the submarine and chased after them.

The four penguins paddled quickly and sped across the water, dodging obstacles as they rushed to get away. "Sir, octopuses at twelve o'clock," said Kowalski.

"Good, it's only quarter past ten," replied Skipper.

As the penguins rowed away, the octopus henchmen used two lamp posts as a slingshot and propelled themselves onto the penguins' gondola.

As Skipper moved into battle stance, the boat zoomed under a washing line and a sock covered his face. "I've lost visual!" he cried. "Kowalski, be my eyes." Skipper swung an oar wildly, hitting one, then two octopus henchmen.

Suddenly, the boat hit a wall and the penguins were thrown through the air. After a wild chase on land, they ended up in an alley with no exit. The octopus henchmen had them surrounded.

"Okay boys, now we spring our trap,"
said Skipper, confidently.

"I'm not so sure that they're the ones that
are trapped, sir," said Kowalski.

Suddenly, an owl swooped down and carried off one of the henchmen.
Then, a baby seal jumped in and took out another, before a polar bear
appeared and zapped the last octopus with a laser. The penguins had
no idea what was happening.

The polar bear, owl and seal all stood in front of the surprised penguins, as a jet soared overhead. From it, a wolf dropped to the ground.

"Don't panic penguins. You are now under the protection of the North Wind," said the wolf. "My name is classified and this is my team. That armoured polar bear is Corporal. The lovely owl is Eva and finally, our explosives expert, Short Fuse. Come along, team, to the jet."

Reluctantly, the penguins followed the North Wind onto their jet. "We have been after Dave for a while now," said Agent Classified, "but we have never been able to get close to him. Tell us what you know."

"We know that he's a whole heap of crazy," said Skipper. "We also know that you and your friends here ruined our trap to catch him."

Agent Classified laughed. "Trap. What trap?" he said. "You were the ones who were trapped."

Skipper puffed out his chest. "Listen up, hot dog. We had things under control," he said.

Agent Classified sniggered while Corporal just stared at the cute penguins.

"We are the elite-est of the elite," boasted Skipper. "The cream of the crop and we don't need you, or your fancy flying machine!"

Agent Classified reached down beside him as Skipper kept talking. "Okay, boys. This is the mission we've been preparing for our entire lives. Penguins are planning this party."

Suddenly, there was a sound, as Agent Classified fired his sleep darts into the four penguins. He smiled, as the four penguins drifted off quietly to sleep.

The penguins awoke to find themselves in the cargo hold of the jet.

"Sir, we're five miles up. Our options are limited," said Kowalski, scanning the area.

"I make my own options," replied Skipper hitting a big, red button with his flipper. An alarm sounded and the cargo doors opened. The penguins and all the North Wind's cargo boxes tumbled out!

The penguins fell through the air, skilfully bouncing from cargo box to cargo box, trying to find something to help them.

Suddenly, they found a bouncy castle. Using Rico like a pump, they inflated it just in time and bounced off, landing safely in a desert. "Right, boys, next stop, civilization to take down Dave," said Skipper, leading the way.

Eventually, the penguins reached the home of the famous Mermaid Penguins at the aquarium in Shanghai, Dave's final target. "Sir, looks like Dave hasn't been here yet. We still have time to stop him," reported Kowalski.

"Now all we need is a man on the inside," said Skipper, looking at Private.

Later that evening, the trap was set. Private was dressed as a Mermaid Penguin while Skipper, Kowalski and Rico waited for Dave. They didn't have long to wait. Soon, Dave appeared and Skipper raced after him.

Suddenly, the North Wind were there, too. Agent Classified and Skipper began to argue over who would bring Dave to justice. Meanwhile, Dave escaped and he took Private with him!

"Private!" cried Skipper, running after Dave. Skipper, Kowalski and Rico got outside just in time to see Dave's submarine disappear under the water. Skipper looked around and saw the North Wind's jet and the three penguins jumped inside.

The North Wind were close behind and saw their jet being taken. "Quick, into this boat!" cried Agent Classified.

Aboard the jet, Skipper was frantically pressing buttons and twisting dials. "Kowalski, how do you steer this thing!" he cried.

"I'm afraid I don't know, sir," replied Kowalski. "We're penguins, we're not supposed to fly."

The jet quickly began to spin out of control and crashed into Agent Classified's boat, leaving the penguins and the North Wind stranded at sea. Together, they slowly followed Dave's course towards his secret island.

As night fell, the two teams located Dave's evil lair and stealthily snuck inside. Just as they were about to take down Dave, an alarm sounded and the room was filled with octopus henchmen.

The penguins and the North Wind were captured. Elsewhere, Private had managed to escape. It was up to him to save his friends and penguin-kind.

Private searched all over the island and soon found his friends and the North Wind locked in a cage. He quickly unlocked it and opened the door.

"Boys, it's time to take care of these slimy sea-dwellers," said Skipper.

The team made their way to Dave's ray machine and jumped into action, bravely fighting the henchmen. Soon, the only octopus left was Dave.

"You're done, Doug," said Skipper.

"My name is DAVE!" cried the octopus.

Private took control of the ray machine, reversed the power and aimed it at Dave. **ZAAPPP!**

Dave had been defeated and the cuteness of all penguin-kind was secured at last.

"Well done, boys, especially you, Private. That's another plan that worked perfectly," said Skipper, smiling.